Gods Among Men

Gods Among Men

Ran Walker

Contents

For Elle

Author's Note

This book was designed to serve as a companion to my collection *Apollo's Toy Box*. While each book may be read separately, the same creative well was present for both.

When the gods wish to punish us, they answer our prayers.

— Oscar Wilde

Part One

Dinosaurs and Baby Shoes

She writes a story about a dinosaur wearing baby shoes, but it's lost on her audience, the dinosaur being a reference to Monterroso's eponymous story, the baby shoes a reference to the apocryphal Hemingway story, both stories under ten words, like her own, and requiring a lot from their readers.

Basquiat

A CAT RESTS upon his lap as he feigns boredom, paint splattered across his pants, his dreadlocks tied up, the old chair slightly uncomfortable, but this will be the image of him they remember most, this black and white photograph capturing his greatness in a way that all true artists seek to be immortalized.

When She Flies Away

He has learned that she can fly when she wants, and this makes him feel threatened, as if a simple argument might lead her to open a window and soar up into the clouds, knowing he cannot follow her to tell her he is sorry (whether he is or isn't), not wanting her to leave him on the earth, alone, staring up into a sky where she is beyond view, his heart aching to be with her, despite his fear of heights.

Strange Toy

THERE WAS something about the doll that was just a little *off*: its eyes asymmetrical, hair wild and wiry, lips a little too pouty, skin mottled. Still, her daughter loved it, playing with it often, embracing the creepiness of the strange toy in the way only a lonely child could.

Spinach

He swirls his tongue behind his lower left second and third molars in a vain attempt to set free a piece of spinach from lunch. She talks incessantly of the "three c's" of diamonds and how her sister got married two years ago and how she had caught the bouquet.

His tongue is now nearly numb from scraping for the spinach, and it dawns on him that she can no more help him with his problem than he can hers.

Euphonium

On a four-valve concert euphonium, the first and fourth valves produce the same sound as the second and third valves. The fourth valve produces the same sound as the first and third valves, and if you want to get really cute, the third valve plays the same as the first and second valves. The math is straight forward; if you can produce the same sum from the valves, you can produce the same sound.

He wonders how a person could invent an instrument that works mathematically this way, and he wonders what other instruments function this way and just how much math influences music. Maybe an instrument like the euphonium was created by a synesthete.

Even more, no one told *him* about the math of this instrument, so then how did he come to understand this? Through experimentation? Through an innate understanding? Through his own synesthesia? Through moving his fingers and blowing through his mouthpiece, exploring the instrument as if he were pioneering a ship across the beautiful chaos of the Pacific?

Lost in the Forest

THEY ARE LOST in the forest, watching the sun set behind trees that may not be trees, ignoring sounds that may not be conversations, feeling trapped within the domain of others, those who were once figments of their imaginations.

The Grand Design
For Steve Jobs

HE BUILT a multi-billion dollar company from his parents' garage and pioneered technology that would one day be ubiquitous, yet as he lay dying, even after a life of creating the unimaginable over and over again, he found himself, in those final moments, so in awe he could only mutter, "Wow. Wow. Wow."

Butterfly

There's a film that he wants to make, though the idea for the film has not revealed itself to him. The keys of his laptop swallow with dry lips. The camera waits with anticipation. The process frozen like wooly mammoths, but eventually things will change. The idea will come and lubricate the gears of the machine, and he will work until the project is done. Until then, he sits, his mind a net, waiting to catch the idea as it flutters about overhead.

Morning Cocoa

He sits a mug of hot cocoa on his desk before he begins to write. He does this instead of coffee, which he has never particularly enjoyed. The temperature outside, of course, is irrelevant. If one could drink coffee any day of the year, one could drink hot cocoa.

He sips, feeling the hot liquid pushing through the whipped cream, and he knows that he will write something good today, something magical.

His Favorite Book

She promised him she would read his favorite book, the one that has sat on her shelf, untouched, for many years.

They are no longer together, but she remains curious as to how the book might've been special to him, though not curious enough to read it.

The Workshop

THE LONE WRITER of color sat helplessly as his MFA workshop cohorts ripped apart his short story. The premise had been simple: a revisionist history in which Africans enslaved Europeans.

The biggest critique? It was too unbelievable (although it was speculative fiction).

His goal was to create empathy.

He'd failed.

We Are the Culmination of Our Experiences

WHEN HE TRAVELED BACK in time, he'd planned to tell his younger self to avoid certain romantic relationships that would only lead to heartache, to avoid certain employers who would stress him, and to avoid poor money choices that would take years to recover from.

But he decided against it.

Pigeons

On the day of their first date, he spent the afternoon getting his hair cut and his car detailed, only to find he was running late for their reservation at Oiseax Affamés, and a dropping of pigeons, true to its name, had splattered his car so heavily he could no longer see it, forcing him to tap at it with a nearby stick, only to find the stick went all the way through to the other side and what had once been his car had now been replaced by a mound of dropping droppings in the shape of his car.

An Audience of One

Every once in a while, he reaches upon his shelf and begins to read one of his older books. The challenge is to see how far he can get into the book before he starts to question some of his decisions. Occasionally, he will get through the entire book and feel it is good, and that book will become his favorite of the books until six months later when he realizes another book is better suited for that designation.

He thinks it is good he can enjoy his own writing and secretly hopes if he ever suffers amnesia during his lifetime, he can pick up one of these books and possibly become his own favorite author.

The Film Students

THE FILM STUDENTS took turns shooting their short horror films in the library, taking advantage of its liminal spaces on the higher floors, the darkness of night dripping through the blinds like black terror-filled tears.

Remarkably, no two films were alike.

Treading Water, Take 1

Sʜᴇ ᴋɴᴏᴡs she will one day drown in media.

She has over 800 unread paperbacks on her shelves. Another 1,500 ebooks sit on her e-reader. There are roughly 100 saved movies on each of her streaming apps and another 75 she purchased. This does not even begin to cover the TV shows she has lined up in her streaming queues.

She has no idea when or if she will be able to get this list of items down to zero, and with new books and movies coming out each week, it is unlikely the list will ever reach that point.

Maybe if she stopped buying new media today, she might reach the end of the list in a decade or so, but that feels rather unlikely.

Her media collection will always be there, and she will be treading water to stay afloat until her arms eventually give out.

Treading Water, Take 2

SHE KNOWS she will one day drown in medias res.

This means she will be in the middle of a book or a film or a TV show when she is suddenly overwhelmed by it all.

Revenge of the Dad, Part 1

HE'D BEEN ASKED if he wanted to use a body double, someone who was a bit more fit. A well-intentioned wardrobe stylist for the video had even recommended a few different shirts that might be more flattering, but the artist was determined to go shirtless, to dance shirtless, to move shirtless, and, on this particular occasion, he had the final word, so when the video starts, the viewer has no choice but to stare at his body in all of its natural glory.

Revenge of the Dad, Part 2

Dad as an adjective is never good.

Dad jokes are often not funny in and of themselves. They are more likely to get a groan than a genuine laugh.

Dad bodies are not considered sexy in and of themselves. They are more likely to get made fun of than appreciated.

Dad shoes are the those big, clunky shoes kids wear when they want to be ironic, until their irony becomes fashionable.

Dad jeans are those jeans that don't have the right cut and look like something a person might wear with Dad shoes once they've given up on trying to look cool.

Dad hats are the relaxed, unstructured hats that are actually shaped by one's head and often get worn backwards with shades by frat boys fresh off the keg.

Maybe Dad is best left as a noun, where it has some actual significance—or at least I hope it does.

Banned, Part 1

THE SMALL GROUP of citizens argued the need to ban books was based on keeping books like *Mein Kampf* and the *The Anarchist Cookbook* from getting into the hands of children. Once they justified the list, they came for Harry Potter, *To Kill a Mockingbird*, *The Bluest Eye*, and *The Hate U Give*, longing to burn those books and become characters like the ones in *Fahrenheit 451* or, better yet, mimic the loyalists who once saluted one of the books originally used to justify the list's existence.

Banned, Part 2

GROWING UP, she was not allowed to read the works of authors who had committed suicide, for fear there would be some nugget embedded deep within the text that might lead her to do the same, but as she grew older, she realized much of the literary canon was filled with gifts from tortured geniuses, as well as those who never knew hunger of any kind, and that each book, regardless of who wrote it or what the life of that writer looked like or how that author's life concluded, offered something unique and special to its reader about how one might navigate the world we collectively inhabit.

Banned, Part 3

First, they banned the dictionaries, then the libraries, then the publishers and writers. Once society had regressed to a collection of sanctioned storytellers and carefully guarded griots, they banned them, too. Now we stand around looking at each other, careful not to offend anyone.

Banned, Part 4

SHE AND HER editor had argued over the multiple uses of the word "fuck" in her book. In one universe, the book was a bestseller. In another universe, the book was a bestseller but banned. In yet another universe, no one even read the book.

Banned, Part 5

Politicians strip history from textbooks to avoid uncomfortable truths.

The National Parks Service creates more historical markers for these stripped, uncomfortable truths.

Meanwhile, we scroll, searching for a truth that suits us.

Part Two

The Gout Chronicles, Part 1

His grandfather called it "walking with Oscar," but he never understood what that meant. "Grouch," his grandfather had said, "rhymes with *gouch*." That didn't help either. His mother had to tell him years later that the word was actually pronounced "gout," and that was the reason his grandfather would sometimes hobble around the house, cursing and complaining about his big toe.

The Gout Chronicles, Part 2

THE DOCTOR TOLD me to drink more water, that pissing clear was how your body expelled the uric acid, that laying off the beef, pork, and shrimp would help. The nurse, in an effort to add some color commentary after the diagnosis, added, "It's funny how you don't think about your big toe until something like this happens."

I started to ask her name, but I already knew it. *Sherlock.*

It had to be.

The Gout Chronicles, Part 3

THERE IS AN ILLUSTRATION OF "THE GOUT," a tiny, rat-like imp that has hooked its claws into a person's big toe. The illustration is dated 1799 and is referred to as the "disease of kings."

I guess anyone can be a king these days.

Good Sleep

HE PONDERS if his sleep has gotten worse over the years or if the anesthesia from his third endoscopy spoiled him on what good sleep could be.

No Words Necessary

His breath was already tilting toward rank when they made love in the twilight hours of the morning, but she chose to ignore it, hoping he'd go to sleep afterwards and spare her any post-coital pillow talk.

Every Game Doesn't Need to Go Into Overtime

She watched his lips moving, though she was now zoned out. Something about a movie he'd seen or something like that. She'd already decided an hour earlier she would sleep with him—but if he kept running his mouth in a quest to meet her where she already was, he might end up talking himself out of a good thing.

The Orange Beanie Club

I HAD a dream where Donald Glover, André 3000, Kendrick Lamar, and I were sitting around in our orange beanies, listening to Coltrane, and wondering if it was better to be a saint or to be knighted. Donald laughed, but didn't share the joke. André blew a light riff on his flute. Kendrick closed his eyes, refocusing on the saxophone. I wrote this story.

Brotha Man Dons His Cape
A Haiku

HE IS FLY when he flies into the deep cyan, headfirst, arms flailing.

Puffer

America has made him into a puffer fish. He swims through life wanting to be unassuming, but racism forms toxins within his skin, building up spikes and spines, making him dangerous if he were to expand.

He doesn't want to expand anymore than Bruce Banner does. He doesn't think America would like him very much if he did. He simply longs to swim in peace, untouched, unprovoked, unassuming, a threat to no one, not even himself.

Robyn

IF WE ARE to believe the celebrities, there is an island flower that smells like heaven, and it is called Rihanna.

Nepotism in the Key of C

Perhaps the moment was simply too big for him. After all, he had been playing the clarinet for only three months.

His aunt had assured him he would be fine to play the national anthem at the volleyball game, but he had his doubts. Still, she, the commissioner of the league, had persisted, telling him he played far beyond his years.

He wanted to believe her, even when his squeaking, coupled with people's random snickering, threatened to return him to a reality he struggled like hell to avoid.

You Cannot Kill Me, Though You May Try

Her publisher loved her first book, but the sales didn't follow, so now he looks at her as one might a bad luck charm or a jinx. Her editor occasionally raves about one of her short stories in an obscure literary journal, but there will be no offers forthcoming. She is damaged goods, her book SKUs skewing her future into uncertainty, but she continues to write, because she refuses to let one book define all that she is and hopes to become.

The Disgruntled Character

SHE IS afraid of the writer.

The writer seems adamant about placing her in horrific predicaments, but she wants to have a simple, uneventful existence.

She understands the idea of conflict, but she does not see herself as a protagonist. She wants to be like the NPCs in video games, where her story is not central to anything of interest to anyone.

But the writer refuses to let her go.

She will be the protagonist whether she wants to or not.

She hopes the writer will remember this before he tells a group of students that characters talk to him and tell him to do these things.

What to Make of a Magnum Opus

The judges of the contest didn't know what to make of her book. The massive collection seemed to include everything except the kitchen sink, and this forced them to discuss whether or not the author did too much with the book, or if the judges were needlessly penalizing the author for writing her magnum opus and having the audacity to submit it to compete against 80-page collections from recently-minted MFA graduates. In the end, out of fear of being on the wrong side of history, they granted the book the award, even though, if they were completely honest, the totality of it was far beyond their—or anybody's—ability to comprehend.

Linus

He remembers the first time he held one of his books in his hands and marveled at how those many pages of a Word document could be transformed into this creative artifact. At that moment, he wasn't concerned about marketing or sales or whether or not the book would earn out on its advance or whether his publisher would ever create another of these beautiful objects from his words. He held the book closely, wanting to savor the moment.

He reflects on this memory, comforting himself like Linus had done numerous times with that baby blue blanket.

Fact vs. Fiction

At times she thought he was writing complete fiction; at other times, she thought he might have been writing nonfiction. It was difficult to tell. After all, weren't books supposed to be one or the other. Were authors even allowed to mix genres within the same work?

As she pondered this, she wondered if it even mattered, and if it did matter, to whom and why? Did it make the pieces less enjoyable or interesting?

Maybe it was all true, except for the parts that weren't, or maybe it was all made-up, except for the parts that weren't.

But couldn't that be said of any book?

Short

He loves when she writes short and is not as much a fan of when she writes long.

It's not that she is completely incapable of writing the longer form. It's that her content works better when written in a shorter form.

It's like a musician who made an decent LP when she could have easily made a great EP.

Black Fist
A Haiku

PROTEST IS the mere act of holding this pen to a single white sheet.

Election Day Morning

ON ELECTION DAY, my brother and I would wake up early to sweep the carpet tacks out of the driveway, the ones left by the bumpkins who figured our father was too *political* for his own good. They couldn't stop us from helping people get to the polls, but they were hoping to at least stall us for a while.

We never missed a single tack, though.

Freedom

As soon as the dissonant organ chords drop, I think of the history being made, Kamala, in her pantsuit, taking the stage, as if shot out of a canon for this ninety-day campaign, because Black women have to have the hardest conditions under which to achieve greatness, my daughter sitting in the passenger seat, as I drive her to school, her chants of "Let me hear my theme song," which is Kamala's theme song, a song that carries with it the weight of history, though it was released prior to the protests of 2020, a song perfect for a time such as this, and Kendrick says, "What you want from me?" as we nod our heads to the weight of the percussion and quote Hattie White like scripture. Amen.

Indecision 2024

He stands there, staring at the blue pair of sneakers and the red pair of sneakers, money in his pockets for only one pair, though he can't decide which ones, but he will decide eventually, and when he does, he will have weighed the pros and cons ad nauseam, exhausted the salesperson, who has run out of helpful suggestions and can now breathe a sigh of relief that she can finally move on to other customers, and we are left to wonder how consequential his choice actually was.

Running

He wakes exhausted from his dreams. He knows insomnia would be no better—probably worse—but he longs for dreamless sleep, or, at minimum, the banality and mundanity of just being a passive observer to the events of his dreams, but dreams aren't like real life. Real life leaves space for wallflowers, while dreams eventually acknowledge you in a way that leaves you exposed and eventually running for your life.

Leitmotifs

53

He knows, before he sits down to write, there will be a story about dreams, a story about purple, a story about a Black body in space. He knows one story will be a version of a previously written story and that there will be several stories with the same titles. He knows, deep down, he is writing the same story—better yet, trying to communicate a common theme—with every effort to put something on the page. He knows all of these things, but he writes anyway because writing is life, and if his life contains these leitmotifs, then so will his work.

Five in a Row

SHE LISTENS to the radio play song after song by her favorite artist, and fear overtakes her, forcing her to grab her phone and do an Internet search.

It is easier for her to believe these songs are a memorial tribute, as opposed to the DJ simply playing *his* favorite artist for the segment.

Pratchett
A Haiku

His DREAMS ARE on his back, like a tortoise holding up the universe.

Part Three

Nocturnal Muse

HE IS FALLING asleep with the words to a poem forming on his tongue. His notebook and phone are across the room, and to get out of bed, he would need to shake loose the coziness of the sleep beginning to envelop him, so he clings to the words, telling himself that he will remember in the morning, that his dreams will not wash these words from his mouth like some type of rinse. He tells himself they will still be there in the morning, willing himself to believe, with his whole heart, in this bit of fiction.

Never Fall in Love With a Vampire
A Haiku

She has decided she will eat him, not love him, against his wishes.

Beyond the Sky

THE SKY above her head feels vast, endless, the clouds occasionally banding together to create images she quickly anthropomorphizes and moves on from, always looking just beyond the blue. It is hard to believe the sky doesn't extend forever. It's like standing on the pier at Buckroe Beach staring at the ocean extending into the horizon. It doesn't feel like she's on a ball spinning in space with blackness that *really* is endless. It feels like she is at the heart of something special, something magical, and all she can do is take it in before it fades away.

On a First Kiss

He is now distracted by her lips, and she is sitting too close to him for him to look away, disinterested. He wants to kiss her, but he doesn't know if she wants him to, so he does not.

Later that night he will go home and wonder if she wanted him to kiss her and wonder if she is wondering why he did not.

Queues

SHE HAS AMASSED a massive queue of horror films over the past several months. Her quest? To watch as many of them as she can from September 1st until October 31st. This is how she brings in the fall each year.

Most of the time she doesn't make it through her list, though. Life doesn't go on vacation, giving her time to watch them all, but she does manage to get to *some* of them, banking the others for next year's even longer queue.

She now understands that her treatment of horror movies is much like her treatment of the books in her personal library and resigns herself to this simple, inalienable fact of life, this endless queueing.

Longhand

When he first began journaling, his hand cramped after each sentence. Once he strengthened his hand enough to write a few pages, he began to teach himself cursive, which at first slowed down his writing a bit, before making his writing both faster and easier. He can now write for more than an hour without cupping his hand and massaging his palm. He doesn't know if his desire to write longhand has made him a better writer, but he does know, without question, it has made him a different writer.

Empty Closet

He stares at the closet, unable to believe how empty it is. She had had more clothes than any sane person needed, so much so that they often fell off hangers or dangled in partially unfolded states, her shoes bunched up on top of each other as if in some Goodwill donation bin. Now she had taken all of those things and put them in the closet of another man, one who apparently had far more space in which to place her belongings.

Sometimes he misses her, but oftentimes he is reminded of all the baggage she carried with her.

Labeling Characters

He writes literary fiction, but his default characters are Black, their descriptions having little to do with their skin color, while his Caucasian characters are described simply as "white." His writing cohort is confused by this and asks why he labels his Caucasian characters this way, but not his Black characters, never once noticing that many of them have inversely done the same thing.

The Book Cover

THE OLD WHITE man looks at the book and says, "There are a lot of people on this cover."

The old white woman looks at the book and says, "There are a lot of men on this cover."

The old Black man looks at the book and says, "There are a lot of white people on this cover."

The old Black woman notices the white men on the cover, but pays them no mind as she looks at all the books on the table.

How It Begins

His blade punctures the pumpkin's flesh with more force than is necessary, and once he has scalped it, he digs out its innards and tosses them onto a newspaper.

He didn't realize it would be this easy to carve up something.

He didn't realize how much he would enjoy it.

October
A Haiku

THE TREE RAINS ITS RED, yellow, and orange leaves down upon the children.

Portraits

You have painted several portraits of me now, and in each one, my eyes are sad. Is this how you see me, this individual burdened by pain that clouds his vision?

I know you say that I am seeing what I want to see, but I do not want to see sadness reflected back at me. It is enough that it tries to eat me from within. Please give me some credit for trying to suppress it when you paint your next portrait. I am doing my best.

Disappearance

THE MAGICIAN MAKES the rabbit disappear, then makes his assistant disappear, then himself. It is only when we try to leave that we realize it is we who have actually disappeared, not them.

Tell Me
A Haiku

TELL ME YOU LOVE ME, even if you have to lie to yourself again.

1,000 Bottles of Baby Oil

IT SOUNDS like the beginning of a nursery rhyme:

"1,000 bottles of baby oil on the wall...take one down, pass it around, 999 bottles of baby oil on the wall."

Actually, the NYC prosecutor used the words "over 1,000," so I guess that makes it worse, and when you consider that was what was left to be seized, that might be even worse.

If this wasn't real, we would laugh, so you probably shouldn't. But if "if" was a fifth, we'd all be drunk.

The Monster in the Closet

The carcass of the monster had lain in the closet so long it no longer emitted an odor, the remains lying in a pile, a disjointed piece of macabre furniture. We kept the door closed most of the time, but the kids would open it to play hide and seek, sometimes climbing within the bones to conceal themselves or to pretend they were devoured by the monster or to imagine the bones were a costume they could animate with their preschool imaginations. The carcass was now a toy, and because they played with it, no one could remember its horror.

The Dog House

75

He has a crook in his neck from sleeping on the recliner, but he will not give her the pleasure of knowing this.

Drying

He still has dreams he is in wardrobe, onstage, seated at the dinner table with three other actors, preparing to give his monologue about refusing to drop out of a political race, and that first word is elusive. He knows if he could nail the first sentence, he could find his rhythm with the rest of his lines. He considers just saying something, freestyling a speech that falls within the parameters of the script. Then he awakens, realizing he's no longer an actor and that when the time had come decades ago, he'd nailed his part—or so he believes.

Purple

Her thighs enveloped him like a fleece blanket, holding his ears in such a way his thoughts were amplified, her moans muffled, and he could no longer tell if he was breathing, but if he was going to die, he would die with her taste coating his tongue like the pocketfuls of grape Kool-Aid he'd once licked from the palms of his hands while wandering the schoolyard.

The Darkest Corner

THE CHAIR SITS, unoccupied, still wet from their bodies, its fabric soaked in ecstasy, the darkness concealing it, as if it were never there.

Infestation

79

SHE TOLD him the bugs in her kitchen were not roaches, but water bugs. She did her best to explain the differences.

To him, though, it didn't matter.

Lollipop

SHE HAD ONCE ALLOWED her boyfriend to penetrate her with a lollypop back when they were in college. Now, she tries not to think of this, as she watches her daughter unwrap a lollipop at the elementary school Halloween party.

Poindexter Zings the Class Bully

WHEN HIPPOS DEFECATE in the water, they wag their tales back and forth to spread it around. Tilapia swim behind the hippo to eat the feces.

Well, T-Bone, your mother is a tilapia.

Metaphors and Similes

SHE IS TORN between whether to use a metaphor or a simile to describe the guy who has just stepped to her:

> *His breath is like a dragon's.*
> *His breath is a dragon's.*

The simile seems to suggest his breath embodies some of the foulness of a dragon's breath, while the metaphor seems to illustrate an embodiment of the dragon's entire foulness. She doesn't know if dragons do, in fact, have bad breath, though, as dragons do not exist. However, Komodo dragons do exist, and they feast off rotted flesh, so maybe the dragon comparison is indeed apt.

Either way, the guy's breath is foul, and in the end, that's pretty much all there is to say about that.

Uncle Joe

THE MEN STOOD in a semi-circle off to the side of the house, a crescent moon beyond the street lamps. They were drunk off muscadine wine, hearts still heavy from interring Uncle Joe earlier that afternoon.

Breaking the silence, one of them told a joke about a guy outsmarting the devil so he could get into heaven, and the others laughed until tears streamed down their faces.

Part Four

The Procrastinator

She had waited until the last minute to write her essay, and the topic her teacher had given her was to write about herself (where does she see herself in five years?), so there was no way she could use AI to write the paper for her, but she refused to accept that fact, so she plugged the USB-C cable into her navel and waited while the cursor blinked on the open document page.

Moment of Clarity
A Haiku

If I forget you in the winter of my life, know that I loved you.

How to Pass the Time During a Zombie Apocalypse

THE ZOMBIE DRAGS a set of chains with it, and I am left to wonder what this means. Zombies typically use their decaying teeth, but this zombie looks as though it would strangle someone. Is it possible for a zombie to strangle someone? Does it possess the fine motor skills and discipline to kill someone in that manner, and if it did, wouldn't that be like playing with its food? I know I will drive a quiver into its skull, but in this barren land, it is fascinating to see something so unusual and to reflect upon it before taking aim.

The Dream That Got Away
A Tanka

SHE TELLS herself she will remember her dream
when she awakens, but those ideas have vanished,
abducted by the sunlight.

Reflections of a Would-Be Superhero

Flying is nice, but humans aren't built to withstand the cold temperatures above the earth.

Strength is cool, but there's only so much you can lift, pull, or push.

Invisibility is where it's at. With invisibility, they'll never ask you to do anything, mainly because they can never find you.

One Day in the Halls of Groverland High

She watches them, hoping they will look up, glance in her direction, give some indication of interest, but they don't. They always seem to be preoccupied with other things, like manga and sketching in their tablet, but this will not deter her. She has decided she will walk over to them and pretend to drop something on the floor at their feet, and they will be forced to look up, and when their eyes meet hers, they will know that she is as special as she believes them to be. She has not allowed herself to think past this point. She has only so much courage to muster at any given time, but she has decided she will use it all on this moment.

Titles

Readers sometimes ask her what the titles of her books mean, and she, in that moment, is forced to make up something to explain the ramblings of her subconscious and make those readers believe there is a greater method to this madness, something intellectual in the center of the absurdity.

Why One Writer Dumped Another Writer

I HAVE BEEN REFLECTING over how to have this conversation. You have clearly expressed promise at times, but I fear you are too heavily influenced by all that is around you, clichés sliding into spaces they shouldn't be. I encourage you to keep trying, as nothing beats a try, but I do hope you find some sense of originality in your work going forward.

The Perks of Being a Microfictionist

WHEN he first began to write stories, he labored over character names and how much exposition to include in his scenes.

When he finally began to write microfiction, these things concerned him far less.

For MF Doom

On Halloween they walk the streets in their *Gladiator* masks, Metal Fingers's instrumentals playing from their portable speakers. They are not trick or treating a la Kubrik; they are forming their own second line, walking the streets of the neighborhood, remembering Daniel Dumile, the supervillain.

My Grandfather, the Dopest Octogenarian

My grandfather walks around wearing Travis Scott x Fragment Jordan 1 highs and lows, name brand sweatshirts and hoodies, and a Gucci sling bag. He listens to my kids' music and often times uses their slang. The irony is that it all feels very natural coming from him, as if this is his authentic style. When I think about it, I am beyond baffled that my grandfather could be a hypebeast, but there are worst things in the world than an octogenarian with a streetwear fetish.

O, My!
A Haiku

SHE WANTS to write a poem about orgasms she has yet to have.

Grief

HE SCREAMS INTO HIS PILLOW, the sound residing only in his head, the rest in the vacuum of space left in his chest, and he feels the world folding in, like origami, on top of him, as he desperately tries to see the sky again.

Cosmic Contracts

"Wʜᴀᴛ's ᴛʜᴇ ᴄᴀᴛᴄʜ?"

"There isn't one."

"What about all this 'throughout the universe in perpetuity' stuff. What does that even mean?"

"It's no big deal. It's standard contract language."

The alien lawyers replayed the recording, now understanding they couldn't claim ownership of the music that had traveled, via sound waves, to their planet.

The Jazz Singer
A Haiku

She scats, not because of Ella, but because she cannot speak English.

Wouldn't You Like to Know

Why don't you name your characters? Don't you worry that your stories feel less personal? Can you really call your pieces stories? Can you really call your pieces poetry?

How would you compare your books to those already in the market? Do you think publishers will be interested in that kind of work? Do you plan to keep self-publishing your work?

How do you market something like that? How many copies of your books do you sell? Do you think you will ever write something more commercial?

What's the end game?

Meshell Ndegeocello

HE LIES ACROSS HIS BED, scribbling on his notebook, while she lies next to him, reading Gloria Naylor, Meshell Ndegeocello playing over the bluetooth speaker softly in the background. The music will eventually lure them away from their pages and invite them to yield to the pending darkness of the room and the hungry embrace of the other.

Black Man Dreaming on TV

THE FIRST EPISODE of season one begins as a dream—but the viewers don't know this yet. The show, after four seasons, will conclude as a dream. True fans of the show will say all of the show's episodes are actually dreams. Occasional viewers will say the show is just too weird and that they stopped watching during season three.

Why Not Make This a Meme?

Unexpectedly, the doppelgängers ran into each other at the neighborhood grocery store. It was the first time all three had been in the same place at the same time. To memorialize the moment, they took a picture of themselves standing in a triangle formation, three Spider-Men pointing at each other.

Slant Reflexions

THEY LOOKED NEARLY IDENTICAL, except one was Black and the other was Caucasian. Their complexions may as well have been miles apart, but there was no denying their features: the same nose, the same jawline, the same smile, the same shaved head, the same broad shoulders.

They were not related, but in that moment, their wives believed otherwise.

Each had once wondered what it would be like to be a different race, and because of this, they stared at each other much longer than would have been considered polite.

Grandfather's Watch

He wears his grandfather's 45 mm watch on his small, frail wrist. He used part of his allowance money to buy a leather strap, since the bracelet was too large to stay on. Even with the strap, though, the watch is massive on his wrist, extending well past his carpal bones. He hopes to one day grow into it, to one day be a hero like his grandfather. Until then he will hold close the only thing he has to remember a man he has only heard stories about.

The Old Woman Next Door

WHEN I WAS an eight-year-old growing up in Mississippi, the old white woman next door would sometimes come out onto her porch and yell disparaging comments at my brother and me for riding our bikes past her house. We never left the sidewalk, never came into her yard, never even slowed down to a speed that could ever be considered loitering, but there she was, fist raised high in the air, voice cackling like a witch on one of the Halloween cartoons we sometimes watched on Saturday mornings. She scared us so badly, we would speed past her house when we were going to the store or coming home.

One day as we were in the process of rushing past her house, I saw my mother standing on the porch of our house, and as soon as the old white woman began to yell, my mother let loose a few words of her own.

After that, the old white woman dared not yell

at my brother and me, and after a while we began to forget that she had ever yelled at us.

Later on, when I was sixteen and shortly after I had traveled abroad to South Korea to attend a Boy Scout jamboree, she saw me cutting the yard one day and approached me. I wondered what she would say, wondered if she would yell at me or say something racist.

I turned off the mower and stood still.

"You went to Korea?" she asked.

"Yes, I did."

"My son went to Korea for the war."

"Yes, ma'am," I responded.

She then turned around and walked back into her house.

She passed away shortly after I went off to college, but that conversation, as brief as it was, stuck with me throughout the years, and while I only had two memories of her, I chose to focus on the latter one.

Dear Jon

SHE MISSPELLED his name on the note she left on his pillow, so he pretended the note was intended for someone else and that she would return.

Gods Among Men

They factored mathematics into their cyphers, architected a fifth pillar of the Culture, and reminded us that we were more than men, yet what passes for Hip Hop these days totally ignores the fact they even exist.

The Last Story

One day he will have written his last story.

He imagines that day will be the day he transitions into energy that was once a writer, but there is a part of him that wonders if it just might be sooner.

Could it be he will have become something altogether different when he leaves the world behind? Maybe a photographer or genealogist? Maybe he will become nothing more than a person who lives each day with a routine as simple as sitting on the swing with his wife and staring at the sunset while they drink Arnold Palmers and reflect on a life well-lived. And if that is the case, that wouldn't be so bad, would it?

Acknowledgments

Thank you to Elle and Zoë, the two halves of my heart.

Many thanks to my family, friends, colleagues, students, and readers. You are appreciated and cherished.

About the Author

Ran Walker (he/him) is the author of 35 books. His short stories, flash fiction, microfiction, and poetry have appeared in a variety of anthologies and journals. Prior to becoming a writer and educator, he worked in magazine publishing and practiced law in Mississippi.

He is the winner of the Indie Author Project's National Indie Author of the Year Award, the Black Caucus of the American Library Association Best Fiction Ebook Award, the Virginia Indie Author Project Award for Adult Fiction, and the Blind Corner Afrofuturism Microfiction Contest. Ran is an Associate Professor of English and Creative Writing at Hampton University and teaches with Writer's Digest University. He lives in Virginia with his wife and much better half, Lauren, and his amazing daughter, Zoë.

Also by Ran Walker

B-Sides and Remixes

30 Love: A Novel

The Last Bluesman: A Novel/(Il était une fois Morris Jones)

Afro Nerd in Love: A Novella

The Keys of My Soul: A Novel

The Race of Races: A Novel

The Illest: A Novella

Bessie, Bop, or Bach: Collected Stories

Four Floors (with Sabin Prentis)

Black Hand Side: Stories

White Pages: A Novel

She Lives in My Lap

Reverb

Work-In-Progress

Daykeeper

Most of My Heroes Don't Appear On No Stamps

Portable Black Magic: Tales of the Afro Strange

The Strange Museum: 50-Word Stories

Bees + Things + Flowers: Microfictions

The World Is Yours: Microfictions

Can I Kick It?: Sneaker Microfiction and Poetry (with Van Garrett)

The Golden Book: A 50-Year Marriage Told In 50-Word Stories

Keep It 100: 100-Word Stories

A Burst of Gray: A Novel In 100-Word Stories

The Library of Afro Curiosities: 100-Word Stories

Black Marker: A Novel in 100-Word Stories

GloKat and the Art of Timing: A Novel in 100-Word Stories

A Different Kind of Christmas Story: A Carol in 100-Word Stories

Spaceships Don't Come Equipped with Rearview Mirrors: 50-Word Stories

This Is Not a Poem/Story: 100-Word Stories

Parts of Speech: 100-Word Stories

Four Suits: A Deck of 100-Word Stories

Oʻahu: Prose Poems

Apollo's Toy Box

Gods Among Men

9 781961 753082